Disclaimer: This is a work of fiction. *Names, characters, businesses, places, events and incidents are either the products of the author's imagination or used in a fictitious manner. Any resemblance to actual persons, living or dead, or actual events is purely coincidental.*

Copyright 2016 by Guardian Publishing Group - All rights reserved.
All rights Reserved. No part of this publication or the information in it may be quoted from or reproduced in any form by means such as printing, scanning, photocopying or otherwise without prior written permission of the copyright holder.

Table of Contents

Chapter 1 3
Chapter 2 32
Chapter 3 56
Chapter 4 84
Chapter 5 111
Chapter 6 135
Chapter 7 160
Chapter 8 191

Chapter 1

Heather shut the back door of Donut Delights behind her and jogged down the steps to her car, which was parked in its usual spot next to the tiny back porch. One of the perks of owning your own business was that sometimes, you could skip out early for lunch with your best friend.

She slid into the driver's seat and flipped the switches on the ventilation system to "Cool" and "A/C On." Ridiculous! She thought. Here it is two weeks before Thanksgiving, and the high temps are still hitting the upper 70's every day.

Not that she wasn't used to it. She'd grown up here in Hillside, Texas, and lived in the same house until she went off to college. College, of course, was where she met Don. They'd dated during their junior and senior years, and then gotten married the week after graduation. Things had been fine for awhile—well, for a few months, anyway—until Don accepted a job offer with a firm in New York City.

Moving to New York City, as a newlywed with Don had brought one shock after another. First, there was the shock of trying to get used to living with Don—who, as it turned out, was nothing like

4

the considerate, understanding boyfriend he'd been while they were dating. Instead, New York City seemed to have changed him into a grasping, controlling, get-ahead-at-all-costs kind of guy.

Or maybe he'd been changing for a long time, and it was just the hustle and bustle of New York City that seemed to bring it to the fore. That, or the extremely cold winters that seemed to bring out the crankiness in everyone. Or the way everyone seemed to mind their own business, and people just didn't reach out to each other the way she was used to.

Or, she sighed, lifting her long, curly red hair off the nape of her neck and then letting it drop, maybe it just wasn't meant to be for Don and me.

They'd hung on for a few years. But finally, they simply realized they'd each become so different from the person they thought they'd married that they just couldn't make it work anymore. After the divorce, Heather had taken her part of the settlement and used it to move back home and start Donut Delights, a shop that sold gourmet donuts, served with coffee and elegance.

Owning her own business had been Heather's dream since

college, but her dream had gotten pushed to the side so that Don could pursue his. It was when Heather finally faced that fact that climbing the corporate ladder had replaced her as Don's dream that she knew the end of their marriage was only a matter of time.

At the sound of a horn honking impatiently behind her, she shook her head to clear out the thoughts of the past and glanced up at the stoplight ahead of her. It was green, and cars from the other two lanes had already moved forward into the intersection.

She tossed a wave at the driver behind her as she pulled forward.

That was enough time spent thinking about the past. The present was much more pleasant, anyway.

She felt her lips curve into a grin that probably looked silly. But so what? She was in love with a man who was very, very different from her ex-husband. Don had been good-looking in a flashy, make-you-take-a-second-look kind of way; Ryan Shepherd's good looks were much more subtle. Or maybe it was simply that Ryan didn't need constant affirmation, or to always be the center of attention.

As a detective with the Hillside Police Department, Ryan spent a lot of time working, as Don had, but only because he wanted to and was good at it. Not because he had to depend on his job to give his life meaning. When his duties interrupted their time together, he always seemed to regret it—and he always made it a point to call, text, or drop by as soon as he could to pick up their meal, or conversation, wherever they had left off.

That's what she wanted—someone who loved her more than he loved his social status or his paycheck.

With Ryan now occupying her thoughts, she didn't notice the police cars parked in front of the shopping center where she was headed until she'd driven into the parking lot. Automatically, her foot hit the brake. What in the world?

She eased off the brake and drove slowly through the parking lot to the dry cleaner's, which had been her destination, a quick errand before she met Amy for lunch. There were several patrol cars parked in the general vicinity of the yellow crime scene tape that blocked off the front of the hair salon next to the cleaner's. And wasn't that Ryan's car? Yes, of course it was.

Heather pulled into a parking spot in front of the cleaner's, stopped the car, got out, and locked up. A uniformed officer exited through the front door of Shear Beauty and headed toward one of the patrol cars. Heather tried to see into the interior of the shop, but she couldn't see much from this angle.

Briefly, she considered walking past the front of the shop, or at least as close as the crime scene tape would allow her. But no, she needed to keep her distance and let Ryan do his job. Besides, he'd call her or text her as soon as he could, anyway.

She pushed open the glass door to the dry cleaner's as a bell tied to the handle jingled. The short, wiry woman behind the counter looked up. "Hello there. You come to pick up your dry cleaning?"

"Yes, please," Heather said. She set her purse down on the counter and dug for her wallet as the woman, whom Heather recognized, but whose name she could never remember, flipped a switch that caused a metal rack with garments hanging from it, bundled together in plastic bags, to begin to slide by.

She located Heather's clothing in short order and brought it to the counter, hanging it on a metal stand. "Do you have any idea what's going on next door?" Heather asked.

The woman frowned. "Oh, no, I don't know. But it must be something pretty bad if all those police officers are out here. And a detective, too. And some other people going in and out."

Probably crime scene, Heather thought, knowing the woman was right. It must be something bad, or there wouldn't be crime scene tape strung across the front of the building. Had someone been murdered?

"I guess we'll read about it in the paper," Heather heard the woman say.

"I guess we will," Heather said. "By the way—what's your name? I'm sorry I don't remember."

"My name is Amala," she said with a smile.

"I'll remember that," Heather said. "I promise. See you next time."

As she stepped through the doorway and back onto the sidewalk, Heather glanced to her right, toward Shear Beauty. Ryan stood on the sidewalk, talking with the same uniformed officer Heather had seen coming out of the salon earlier. Ryan glanced up, and their gazes met. Heather gave him a small smile and nodded at him as she continued walking toward her car. One corner of Ryan's mouth twitched upward briefly before his expression became businesslike again and he turned back to the patrolman.

Despite the curiosity that was driving her crazy, she knew she had done the right thing. Her willingness to wait for the information she desired would give him the chance to do his job. It would also show him that she had confidence in him and in their relationship.

And she did have that confidence, she realized as warmth filled her chest and suffused her cheeks. Their's was the kind of relationship she had always wanted. And Ryan was the man she'd been looking for.

***

She didn't have much time to ponder her new realization, however, or what it might mean for the future, because the Mexican restaurant at which she was meeting Amy was only 5 minutes away.

The best parking spot she could find was on the side of the restaurant, halfway down the row. She wasn't surprised; Dos Chicos was a popular eating spot, and 12:00 noon was right in the middle of the lunch rush.

Heather grabbed her purse, got out, locked up, and started the trek to the front door. Maybe getting some exercise both before and after their meal would help to offset the huge calorie load she planned on ingesting.

She pulled open the heavy, wooden front door and stepped inside. The black, faux-leather benches in the space between the outer doors and the inner ones were empty, which surprised her. She'd expected to see them full of hungry customers waiting for a table.

When she pulled open the second door and entered the main part of the restaurant, however, she found the benches there occupied by several couples as well as a group of businessmen in dress shirts and ties.

A smiling hostess returned to her wooden stand just as Heather approached. "How many in your party?"

"Two, please."

"Your name?"

"Heather."

The hostess noted Heather's name on the list. "It should be about fifteen minutes," she said.

"That's fine," Heather agreed. As she turned to survey the seating options, one woman slid a little closer to her husband so that Heather could sit down next to her on the bench.

"Thanks," Heather said.

Twelve minutes later, when the hostess called her name, Amy still hadn't arrived. Heather wasn't surprised. Amy was frequently late, especially when they weren't attending an event that started at a specific time, and Heather had learned to make allowances for that.

The hostess led her to a table in the middle of the dining room.

Heather sat down in a chair facing the entrance so that she could watch for Amy, as the hostess placed a menu in front of her. "Your server will be right with you," she said, before returning to her duties at the hostess stand.

Heather didn't bother to open the menu. She knew what she wanted because she always got the same thing when she ate at Dos Chicos: the enchilada plate, with three enchiladas topped with cheese and gravy, the best Mexican rice she had ever tasted, and refried beans.

"Hello. How are you today?" The waiter stopped next to her table and placed one glass of water in front of her and the other at Amy's place.

"I'm fine, thank you," Heather said, removing the slice of lemon from the rim of the glass. "How are you?"

"Doing well, thank you. I see you're waiting on someone?"

"Yes. She should be here any minute."

"Can I bring you anything while you wait? An appetizer, perhaps?"

"No, thanks. Just the chips and salsa. Two bowls of salsa, please."

"No problem. I'll be right back." The waiter smiled, then headed toward the kitchen.

He was back in two minutes with a basket lined with white paper and filled with triangle-shaped tortilla chips, and two small, black pots of salsa. "Here you go," he said, arranging the food on the table.

"Thanks," Heather said. She glanced toward the front door and saw Amy making her way toward them. The waiter saw her, too, and waited until she got close enough to hang her purse over the back of the chair.

"May I get you something to drink?"

"Just the water will be fine for now," Amy said.

"Would you ladies like a couple minutes to decide?"

"I would, please," Amy said, settling into her chair.

"Then I'll be back in a few minutes." With what Heather by now assumed was his trademark smile, he went to check on another table of customers.

Amy leaned forward over the table, as close to Heather as she could get. "Okay, spill it," she said.

Heather frowned. "Spill what?"

"Why was there yellow crime scene tape around Shear Beauty when I showed up for my appointment this morning?"

"I don't know." Heather shrugged. "I don't know everything that goes on in Hillside, you know."

Amy picked up her white napkin-wrapped bundle of silverware and pointed it at Heather. "But your boyfriend is a detective."

"I haven't talked to him about it yet," Heather said, watching Amy pick up the salt shaker and shake a ridiculous amount of salt onto their basket of chips. "I went to pick up my dry cleaning, and I saw that something was going on. But I don't know what."

"Well, you'll have to tell me as soon as you find out." Amy dipped a chip into her pot of salsa, bit off the corner with the salsa on it, chewed, and swallowed. "Anyways, I have some great news. I have a date tonight! I just need to find a new hairdresser in time."

"Oooh! With whom?" Heather asked.

"You've never met him," Amy said, waving her hand as if brushing the topic away. "He's just a guy I met at my last art show. No big deal."

"No big deal, but you just have to have your hair done for tonight?"

"Well…yes. I mean, just because this isn't any big deal doesn't mean I don't want to look my best."

"That's the second time you've said this was 'no big deal,'" Heather said, raising her eyebrows and watching Amy try to look nonchalant. "'Methinks the lady doth protest too much.'"

"Well, I mean, it's just Chris."

"'Just Chris?' Does 'just Chris' have a last name?"

"Bennett," Amy said. "Chris Bennett." She glanced around the restaurant, as if trying to find something else to talk about.

"Amy, come on. This is me, remember?"

"I know," Amy said, suddenly looking miserable. "Okay, I give. Chris is a big deal."

"That's great!" Heather said. "Isn't it?"

"I don't know," Amy said. "I just really like him. More than I've liked any guy in a really long time."

"So what's the problem?"

Amy shrugged. Her brown eyes seemed to be struggling to meet Heather's gaze. "I guess I'm just afraid this relationship will turn out like all the other ones. Gone. Finished. Kaput." She sighed. "And I really want this one to last."

"Do you think Chris is 'the one?'" Heather asked.

"I don't know," Amy said. "But I think he might be."

The first notes of "Here Comes the Sun" floated out of Heather's purse. She ignored the ringtone. "That's awesome, Amy," she said. "You deserve somebody who's just as wonderful as you are."

"Thanks," Amy said.

"So is he wonderful?" Heather asked with a smile.

Amy smiled, too. "He's amazing," she said simply.

"So you need to get your hair cut before tonight, before your date with The amazing Chris. You want the name of the girl I go to? I'm sure she'd try to squeeze you in today if there's any way she can."

"Maybe. I just wonder how much longer Shear Beauty is going to be closed. I've been going to Kelly for 10 years. I don't really want to switch."

"Here Comes the Sun" had stopped playing several seconds ago. Now, the notification tone went off on Heather's phone. "Just let me check that a sec," she said, reaching into her purse. She withdrew her phone, saw that she had received a text, and read it. Oh, no.
"What's the matter?" Amy asked.

Heather looked up from the phone screen to meet Amy's eyes. "I think you better plan on finding another hairstylist," she said. "Not just today, but...forever."

"Why? What's the matter with Kelly?"

The words seemed unreal even as they rolled from her lips. "She's dead," Heather said.

Chapter 2

Heather's doorbell was one of those old-fashioned ones where it rang as long as you turned it. Most people usually caused it to produce one long ring. But when three short rings sounded, she knew that it was Ryan at the door.

Shucking both her oven mitts onto the counter, she glanced at the table, where she'd just set the lasagna in the midst of two place settings next to a glass dish of garlic-and-parmesan green beans. Oh! Spoons!

She grabbed two serving spoons from the silverware drawer and stuck one in the corner of the lasagna pan and the other in the dish of green beans. No, wait. A spatula. She whirled back toward the drawer just beneath the silverware drawer, yanked it open, and snatched out a spatula. Exchanging it for the lasagna spoon, she tossed the spoon toward the sink and heard it clatter in as she hurried toward the front door.

Ryan stood on her wide, wraparound front porch, holding a bouquet of flowers wrapped in green florist's paper. Yellow and orange blooms peeked from the top of the spray, surrounded by oak leaves in hues of green, orange, and dark red. As he stepped inside, he handed her the bouquet.

"Thank you," she said, surprised. "To what do I owe this royal treatment?"

"To the fact that I didn't start treating you royally soon enough," Ryan said.

"Well, thank you," she repeated, her tongue suddenly feeling thick and awkward. "Let me just put these in some water."

She headed for the kitchen with Ryan following, then busied herself locating a vase beneath the sink, running water in it, and plunking the flowers in. "This looks delicious," Ryan said from behind her.

She turned and found him eyeing the lasagna. "Everything will be ready in a few minutes," she said. "We're just waiting on the garlic bread."

"I can't wait," he said. "Need help with anything?"

"No thanks," she said, setting the vase of flowers on the ledge that divided her kitchen from her living room. "Getting the garlic bread out of the oven is a one-person job. Have a seat."

Ryan pulled out a chair and sat down. "You expect me to sit here without eating this?" he teased, pointing to the lasagna.

"Yes, I do," she said. "Patience, sir, patience." She flipped on the oven light and glanced inside at the foil-wrapped loaf of French bread she'd prepared earlier with liberal amounts of garlic and butter.

"I've been patient all day," Ryan groaned. "I wanted to see you."

"Well, now you see me," she said, spreading out her hands, palms up. "Here you are, and here I am. Now what?"

The next thing she knew, she was caught up in Ryan's

embrace, his lips finding her's. She returned his kiss for a moment, then stepped back. "Three minutes," she said.

Ryan looked bewildered. "What?"

"Three more minutes on the garlic bread. We don't want it to burn."

"I don't care if it burns," Ryan said, drawing her back toward him and attempting to cover her lips with his own. "I don't care if the fire department has to come put it out. I—"

"Well, I do," she said, smiling, teasingly pushing him away. "I love garlic bread. Not that I need any more carbs after all the carbs I ate at lunch."

Ryan flopped back into his seat. "You had lunch with Amy?"

"Yep. Dos Chicos."

"I missed lunch today."

"Working on the murder at Shear Beauty?" she asked.

"Yeah." Ryan paused, then shook his head.

"What happened?"

"There's not much I can tell you on this one," Ryan said. "Only what you're going to read in the paper or what you probably already heard on the news."

"I didn't watch the news. What would I hear? Or read in the paper?" She glanced at the oven timer and saw it counting down the seconds in the last minute. Heather put on one of her oven mitts, opened the oven door, and pulled the tray of garlic bread out. She set it on the stovetop, took off the oven mitt, and began gingerly picking apart the aluminum foil along the seam she'd made when she wrapped it.

"Kelly Carlson was bludgeoned to death in her shop," Ryan said.

"Her assistant found her this morning when she got to work."

"When was she killed?" Heather asked, placing several slices of garlic bread in a silver bread basket.

"Probably last night."

"Any idea who did it?"

"We're checking out a possibility," he said.

"Which you can't tell me about?" Heather asked, sitting down across from him.

"Right."

"Okay," she said. "Just tell me whenever you can."

"I will," he said. "Thanks for understanding."

She smiled at him in response. "Want some lasagna?"

"I thought you'd never ask," he sighed. He held his plate for her as she cut and served him a large piece with the spatula, then used her clean fork to cut the strings of cheese that led from his plate to the baking dish and pile them on his lasagna.

As Ryan served himself green beans and garlic bread, Heather filled her plate as well, taking a small piece of the lasagna as a concession to lunch's caloric excess. "Mmm, these beans are delicious," Ryan said around a mouthful.

"Thanks," she said. "Just a little olive oil and garlic, a little parmesan cheese, and voila."

"This is better than Giovanni's," he said, referring to the restaurant they most frequently patronized. "Better than my lasagna, too."

"You cook? Why did I think you didn't like to cook much?"

"Because I don't," he said. "But that's not because I can't cook.

I'm actually a great cook. It's just that I don't have a lot of time to spend in the kitchen. And somehow, it doesn't seem worth it to go to a lot of trouble for just one person."

"I know what you mean," she said.

"Our next date," he said, punctuating his words with jabs of the fork toward her, "I'll cook for you."

"You're on," she said. "What's your specialty?"

"You'll have to wait and find out," he said, as a whine sounded from right next to the table. They both glanced toward the floor to see Dave, Heather's fluffy, white mixed-breed dog, looking up at Ryan with pleading eyes. "No way, Dave," Ryan said. "This is mine. Dogs don't eat lasagna, anyway."

"Um, actually," Heather said, giving him her best guilty look, "they do, sometimes."

"Dave eats lasagna?"

"And Chinese food. Except he doesn't like vegetables. Just the meat."

"A dog after my own heart," Ryan said. "But he's still not getting my lasagna."

"Don't you ever let Bella eat anything besides cat food?" Heather asked.

Now it was Ryan's turn to look guilty. "We're talking about Dave," he said with mock seriousness. "You leave Bella out of this."

"That's what I thought," Heather said smugly, and dug into her meal.

***

That night, after Heather had let Dave out into the backyard, waited for him to do his business, and let him back in, she walked into the living room and picked up the remote. "It's okay, Dave," she said to her dog, who was looking at her with his head cocked to one side, the way he always did when he didn't understand some departure from their normal routine. "I just want to watch part of the news. Probably just the first part."

Heather took up her favorite position on the couch, slouching low against the cushions with her feet up on the coffee table in front of her, and pushed the button to turn the TV on. She had to wait through the opening graphics and intro before the scene changed to show the two news anchors sitting at their desk and looking seriously into the camera.

"At the top of the news tonight," Jane Duvall said, each blond hair perfectly in place and makeup highlighting her flawless features, looking every bit the beauty queen she had once been, "is the story of the murder of a Hillside businesswoman."

As she continued, the camera cut to an exterior shot of Shear Beauty, showing the yellow crime scene tape and an officer standing guard. "Kelly Carlson was the owner of Shear Beauty, a popular hair salon on Lakeridge Road. This morning, she was found bludgeoned to death in her shop when her assistant arrived for work. Police do not yet have a suspect, but they are following up on potential leads. And they—and the victim's family—are asking for the public's help in solving this crime."

Then, suddenly, Ryan's face filled the screen above the words Detective Ryan Shepherd, Hillside PD. Someone off-camera was holding a microphone for him. "We can't release very many details at this time," Ryan said. "We're still very early in the investigation. However, we were able to notify Ms. Carlson's family this morning, and they have asked us to release her name and to ask anyone who has any information regarding this crime to please contact the Hillside Police Department."

Heather snatched up her phone and tapped out a text—You're you're on television!—and pressed "send.".

"We will keep you updated as this story unfolds," Jane Duvall said, wrapping up. "Brad?" She turned to her co-anchor, who now held a sheaf of papers in front of him as he launched into the next story.

Heather's phone pinged with an incoming message. She read it and smiled.

I hate being on television.

"Okay, Dave, that's it," Heather said, pointing the remote toward the TV and turning it off. "That's all I needed." Dave stood up from his doggie bed in the corner, waited for her to check to make sure the front door was locked and then turn off the lights, and followed her down the hall toward her bedroom.

As she changed into flannel pajama pants and a T-shirt, Dave jumped up onto her bed and curled up into a sleepy ball. "So it's my bed tonight, is it?" Heather asked. "Okay, stay there."

She headed into the tiny bathroom off her room, turned on the water, and waited for it to get warm so she could wash her face. Even though she rarely wore makeup, she still made it a point to go through the ritual of cleansing her face every night. It was good for her skin, and besides, the warm water was a nice, relaxing touch as she readied herself for bed.

When she had hung her washcloth back up, she squeezed toothpaste onto her toothbrush and began to brush her teeth, staring at her reflection in the mirror. Something was niggling at the back of her mind. What was it?

Bludgeoned inside the shop. That was it. Kelly Carlson had

been bludgeoned inside her shop. That meant she had probably known her killer—or at least let him or her in.

Or maybe the killer just walked through the front door, Heather told herself, playing devil's advocate. Maybe the killer was a customer.

Heather spit her mouthful of toothpaste foam into the sink. The police were probably checking out all of Kelly's customers from yesterday, she realized, or at least the evening customers, to see if one of them might have killed her.

But somehow, she had a feeling the police wouldn't find any useful information by pursuing that possibility. It seemed more likely that the killer wouldn't be on Kelly's appointment book. Which led Heather back to the probability that Kelly had known her killer and let the person in. Because whether the killer had been present in the shop and had stayed after the last customer left, or whether Kelly had let him or her in later, the fact remained that she probably wouldn't have done either of those two things without knowing the person.

Heather sighed as she turned off the bedroom light and slipped between the covers of her bed.

Sometimes, she really didn't envy Ryan having to figure things out.

Speaking of Ryan...

She felt her cheeks heating up and knew that if anyone could have seen her at that moment, they would have seen her blushing as she wondered what it might be like to be married again and to share a bed with Ryan someday.

She turned over to face the empty side of the bed. What would it be like to have someone sleeping on a pillow right next to her? She'd have to move out of the middle of the bed, of course, and only take up her half.

Heather scooted over to the side of the bed nearest her nightstand. She lay there for a minute and decided she could live with sleeping on only one half of the mattress.

But what about other practical considerations? she She wondered. Did Ryan snore? Did he hog the covers?

She turned back onto her other side, facing the nightstand this time as she always did, and smiled.

One day, perhaps, she would find out the answers to those questions.

Chapter 3

Even before Heather picked up the morning paper in its plastic sleeve from her front porch, she could see the large-font, bolded letters of the headline. She took the paper back inside, closed the door behind her, and shook the rolled-up tube from the plastic wrapper. Unfolding it, she read, "Local Woman Found Bludgeoned to Death."

She carried the paper into the kitchen and sat down at the table. Holding the paper up with one hand, she gripped the handle of her coffee cup with the other and raised the mug to her lips.

Taking her first sip of the brew, she began to read.

"Yesterday morning, 28-year-old Hillside resident Kelly Carlson was found bludgeoned to death inside her hair salon, Shear Beauty. Ms. Carlson had been a resident of Hillside for 5 years. Her body was found this morning by her assistant, Rachel Goodman, when Ms. Goodman arrived for work.

Police say Carlson was killed sometime the night before. At this time, they are not releasing any details about potential suspects. The Hillside Herald has learned, however, that arrests have been made in the vicinity of Shear Beauty the night Carlson was killed. Three juveniles were taken into custody for possession of marijuana and possession of a firearm. Their names are not being released because they are minors."

Hmm, she thought. Interesting. Could the three teenagers have killed Kelly? True, she hadn't been shot, but maybe they'd pistol-whipped her and gone too far.

But why would they have attacked her inside the shop? Why would they have been inside late at night, and what motive could they have had for the attack?

On TV, it's always money or love, she thought. Assuming it wasn't love—because that just doesn't sound right—could it have been money? Maybe they knew Kelly was closing up shop and probably had some cash on hand from the day's proceeds?

Maybe so. But that still left the matter of how they had gotten inside. Of course, Kelly may very well not have felt threatened by three teenagers. She may have either let them in after the door was locked, or let them stay after the last customer left.

But wasn't marijuana supposed to make people mellow? Wasn't it usually people who were hopped up on crack or something that went around killing people, not people who were high on pot?

The one time Heather had tried pot had been long ago, when she was in high school herself. She hadn't felt like doing anything violent. In fact, it had seemed like a great idea to lie on her back on her friend's sofa and contemplate the meaning of life and of the ceiling tiles. So, yeah, it wasn't likely that the teenagers had smoked a joint, and then attempted to rob and kill Kelly. Of course, maybe they hadn't been high at the time.

"Aarrggh," Heather groaned out loud in frustration. Nothing about this seemed to make sense, and Ryan had said he couldn't tell her much this time.

It wasn't even really her business to try to figure things out. And she certainly wasn't a professional. But her overactive curiosity gene wouldn't allow her to let the mystery go. Any mystery, for that matter. And this one was more important than most, because a young woman had lost her life.

Scratching at the back door alerted her that Dave wanted back in. She opened the door for him and contemplated, for the thousandth time, having a doggie door installed. But her friend Kathleen had had one put in, and Kathleen's dog wouldn't even use the door. He was afraid of it, Kathleen said.

"Guess I'll just keep letting you in, Dave," Heather said, pouring some kibble into Dave's bowl next to the refrigerator. She picked up his water bowl, dumped the water out in the sink, and filled it with fresh water. "Here you go," she said, setting it down next to his food. Dave took a couple of perfunctory laps from it, and then went back to crunching his kibble.

She glanced at the clock on the microwave, saw that it was 7:02, and decided she might as well get ready for work. She'd woken up early that morning—well, early for her, at least. She normally didn't get up until 7. But her employees—Maricela, Angelica, Jung, and Ken—arrived at Donut Delights at 3 a.m.

Heather shuddered just thinking about having to be up that early on a regular basis. Even doing it for just a couple days when Maricela and Angelica had to miss work for a death in the family a couple months ago had made her desperate for sleep. And even more grateful than she already was for her fantastic employees who, over the months or years they had worked for her, had become like family.

***

Sure enough, when she came through the back door of her shop into the kitchen at 7:45, the four of them were hard at work making donuts and serving customers. She dropped her purse in the bottom drawer of her desk in her tiny office and turned back toward the kitchen.

Grabbing a hairnet, slipping it over her hair, and tying on an apron, she joined Ken at the counter, where he was cheerfully filling customers' orders for donuts. Jung worked alongside him, but Heather knew Jung preferred to make donuts rather than help run the register.

"I've got it. You can go see if Maricela and Angelica need anything," Heather said.

"Thanks," Jung said. "Holler if you need me."

For the next thirty minutes, Heather and Ken were kept busy serving the customers who arrived in a steady stream, ordering donuts, then lingering at the wrought iron tables and chairs as they enjoyed a brief respite from their busy lives. When the pace began to slow down, Heather grabbed a coffee pot and circulated among the tables, refilling people's cups.

Interacting with her customers was Heather's favorite part of her job. To her, that's what owning a business was all about, providing her customers with an experience where they felt that not only their money was valued, but they were valued. And you just couldn't communicate that if you stayed behind the counter all the time.

When she'd refilled everyone's cup that wanted a refill and brought two more donuts to a couple who had decided to try another gourmet flavor, Heather slipped back into the kitchen.

"Everything okay back here?" she asked.

"Everything's fine," Ken said. "Actually, I have something for you."

"For me? What is it?"

"I'll get it," Ken said. He walked over to the employees' lockers that were tucked in the back corner of the kitchen and came back carrying something on a tray. "It's a coffee cake," he said, presenting it to her. "My wife made this to thank you for hiring me on permanently."

"That was nice of her," Heather said, accepting the platter, "but she didn't have to do that. You're an amazing employee. I'm lucky to have you."

Ken ducked his head and smiled. "I told her you knew how to bake," he said, "but she insisted."

"I know how to make donuts," Heather said. "I don't know how to bake. Big difference." She glanced at the front counter and saw there was no line of customers waiting. "Let's take this into my office, and everyone can have a piece. Somebody grab napkins and a knife, will you?"

They all crowded into the office that wasn't really big enough for five people but somehow held them all. Heather cut slices of the coffee cake and passed them out. When each of her employees had one, she served herself a piece and took a bite.

"Oh, my goodness!" she exclaimed as the buttery cinnamon flavor rolled across her tongue. "This is fantastic!"

"Thank you," Ken said. "I'll tell her you said that."

"Tell her I need the recipe," Heather said. "We need to turn this into a donut."

"How are you going to turn it into a donut?" Ken asked.

"Mmm," she said, licking her lips to catch any stray traces of brown sugar. "We start out with a medium-weight cake donut and top it with chopped pecan crumbles and a brown sugar-cinnamon-butter glaze. We can call them Cinnamon Crumbles."

"You're going to make a donut from my wife's recipe?"

"If she doesn't mind," Heather said.

"Mind? She'll be thrilled."

"Great," Heather said, taking another bite of coffee cake and rolling her eyes toward the ceiling. "Mmm. Okay, I better get back out front before I sit down in here and eat this entire thing myself."

As she approached the glass cases where they displayed the luscious donuts for sale, the door opened, and a group of teenagers walked in, chattering and laughing. Heather glanced at the clock and saw that it was 8:30. Hadn't school already started? Well, maybe not.

"Good morning. What can I get for you today?" she asked with her friendliest smile.

But even as she filled their order, her mind wasn't on the donuts they chose or the drinks they purchased. Instead, her thoughts were focused on another group of teenagers she hadn't even met. Teenagers with a gun and some drugs. Teenagers who might have killed Kelly Carlson.

***

Heather wasn't sure what made her decide to take a break and drive past Shear Beauty. It wasn't as if she thought she could find some clue that the police had missed. But something—that curiosity gene again?—prompted her to head down Lakeridge and turn in to the parking lot.

The yellow crime scene tape was gone, which didn't surprise her. She figured the police would have gotten everything they needed before they ever left yesterday. Pulling into a parking spot directly in front of Shear Beauty, Heather put the car in park and sat there thinking. It probably wouldn't hurt for her to get a glimpse inside. Despite having patronized the dry cleaner next door for years, she'd never been into the salon.

Heather got out and stepped up onto the sidewalk. Would anybody think it was strange for her to be there? No, they'd probably just think she didn't know the shop was closed.

Maybe they'd think she had an appointment to get her hair done.

She approached the plate glass window on which bright orange and yellow window art proclaimed Special! Ladies' hair cuts $20. Men's $15. Children's $12. Cupping her hands around her face, she leaned toward the window until her nose touched the glass and peered inside.

It looked just like any other hair salon she had ever seen. There were two sinks, two client chairs and stylist workstations, and two hair dryer chairs. Black plastic chairs with metal legs where customers could sit and wait for their turn lined the front wall on either side of the door. A coffee table held magazines. A plastic plant stood in one corner.

Heather jumped as a young woman came out of what Heather assumed was the stock room carrying a bag. "We're closed!" the young woman called out, her voice faint through the glass.

"I don't want a haircut," Heather said, trying to strike a balance between making her voice audible to the employee and not broadcasting her business to anyone who might be walking by.

"I just want to ask you something."

The young woman came to the front door, turned the lock, and opened the door a crack. "We're closed," she repeated. "Sorry."

"I know," Heather said. "I know what happened here. I just had a question."

"What's your question?"

"Could I come in?" Heather asked.

At first, the young woman hesitated, and Heather thought she was going to tell her to go away. But then the woman stepped back, pulled the door open further, and allowed Heather in. "Let's go in the back room," she said. "I don't want anyone to see us talking and think we're open."

Heather followed her into the stock room, where the light was already on. "I'm Heather Janke," she said.

"I'm Lisa," she said. "Lisa Giddings. Look, I'm not sure how you think I can help you, but I didn't want to try to have this conversation through the front window."

"I appreciate that," Heather said. "I was just wondering...are you still going to keep the shop open?"

Lisa shook her head. "Nope. It wasn't my shop. I just worked for Kelly. It's up to her family what they want to do with it. They said they're thinking about it. So right now, I'm out of a job."

"Could you set up your own salon?"

"If I had the money," she said. "But I don't have anyone to get me started in business like Kelly did."

"Do you know if Kelly had any enemies?" Heather asked. "Somebody who hated her enough to do this?"

"I don't know," Lisa said, shrugging. "I mean, I guess nobody gets along with everybody."

"Any unhappy customers?"

Lisa's eyes narrowed. "Why do you want to know all this?" she asked. "Are you with the police?"

"I just wanted to see if Shear Beauty was going to stay open," Heather said. "I figure if Kelly's customers were pretty happy with her, then her family might consider reopening the shop. I know my friend Amy Givens came to Kelly for years. She loved Kelly's work."

"Oh, you're Amy's friend?" Lisa asked. "I know Amy. Kelly cut her hair, but I knew her. She was always so much fun to talk to. I'll miss her. Actually, I'll miss all the customers. Except Lana Sturmer."

"Lana wasn't one of your nicest customers?" Heather probed.

"To say the least," Lisa said, rolling her eyes. "Every time she came in here, she acted like she was queen of the world or something. She was so full of herself and that daughter of her's. Emily competed in beauty pageants. I think she might have even won a couple. Lana always brought her here to get her hair done before a pageant. And believe me, everything had to be just perfect, or it would be our fault her Emily didn't win."

"No pressure," Heather said.

"I know, right? Emily was as sweet as could be. But not Lana. Kelly spent way more time on Emily's hair than she should have to, just to make sure Lana was satisfied. And Lana left here happy every time. Even the last time Kelly did Emily's hair, Lana was happy with it. But then she came in the next day and started screaming at Kelly in front of the other customers. Apparently, Emily only got runner-up, and Lana said it was all Kelly's fault."

"Why didn't Kelly just fire Lana as a client?"

"That's what I wondered. But she never did. Well, I guess Lana will have to find another hairstylist to yell at now." Lisa's face was suddenly sad. She clamped her lips together, and Heather saw tears in her eyes.

"I didn't mean to upset you," Heather said. "I'm sorry. I hope things work out, either here, or wherever you decide to work next."

Lisa nodded, barely looking at her.

"I'm sorry for your loss," Heather said. Lisa sniffled and turned away.

Heather walked quietly to the front door of Shear Beauty and let herself out.

Chapter 4

When Heather made it back to Donut Delights, she'd been gone much longer than she'd anticipated. "Sorry I was gone so long," she said as she hurried in through the back door.

"No problem," Jung said, hooking a thumb back over his shoulder towards the dining room. "You have a visitor."

Heather stepped forward, craning her neck so she could see into the dining room. She spotted Ryan sitting at a table near the window, leaning toward...Eva?

At that moment, her favorite customer looked up and smiled. Heather saw her say something to Ryan, and then Ryan turned and caught sight of her.

Wait a minute. Was that a guilty look on his face? Why would he feel guilty about sitting and chatting with an elderly woman whose friendship he knew Heather enjoyed?

But the guilty look was gone, replaced by the smile she loved so much. Ryan stood up and met her at the counter. "Hey, Beautiful. I was hoping you'd be back soon. I only have a minute left before I have to get back to work."

"Hey, yourself," she said. "Busy day?"

"Yep. Would you mind bagging up a couple donuts for me to take with me?"

"A cop eating donuts?" Heather teased. "Who ever would have thought?"

"It's something they teach us in the academy," Ryan said.

"Donuts 101."

Heather laughed. "What flavors do you want?"

"Whatever's good today."

She glanced down her nose at him, which was harder to do since he was several inches taller than she was. "Everything's good," she said.

"Of course it is," Ryan said. "My bad. Just give me two of whatever you recommend."

"Any new developments you can tell me about?" she asked, carefully placing a Southern Pecan Pie donut in a bag.

"Make it two of those," Ryan said.

"Those look great."

"Okay," she said.

"As for what I can tell you, I can say that we're waiting on autopsy results for answers to some questions. Can't say much more than that."

"Did you know about Lana Sturmer having an argument with Kelly?"

"We know. The question is, how do you know?"

"I drove by Shear Beauty, and Lisa was there," she answered.

"I asked her if the shop was going to stay open. I was curious on Amy's behalf. Amy's gotten her hair done there for years. Once Lisa found out I knew Amy, we got to talking about the murder, and she told me."

"Just be careful," Ryan said. "We need room to do our jobs. And I don't want you to get hurt."

"I wasn't trying to do your job," Heather said. "I was there, we were talking, and I asked a few questions."

"I know," Ryan said with a sigh.

"I know."

"Is there something wrong with what I did?" A frown creased Heather's forehead.

"I'm not sure this is the place to be having this discussion," Ryan said.

"Then let's go have it in my office."

"Right now?"

"Right now."

Ryan walked around the end of the counter and followed her to her office. She closed the door behind them, and they both sat down. She plunked the bag with his donuts onto the desk next to him. "So what's going on?" she asked.

He leaned forward, forearms on his knees, gaze directed at the floor. His classic "thinking" pose. She waited for him to speak. In a moment, he looked up, and his eyes met hers. "You're not a professional," he said. "If you get involved with a murder investigation, it could compromise the perceived purity of the evidence and the impartiality of the investigation."

"What? I wouldn't compromise any evidence."

"You wouldn't mean to," Ryan said. "But a good defense attorney could look at the fact that you're my girlfriend, and I knew you were investigating. He could claim that I was encouraging you to act in an official police capacity, which would get me in a lot of trouble. He could also claim that witnesses' testimony was improperly influenced or even improperly gained because you don't know what you're doing."

"So what am I supposed to do if I'm talking to somebody, and the topic of the case comes up? Just stop talking about it?"

"Ideally, yes," Ryan said. "If the person has any information, that is. You could tell him or her to come to me directly. I know what I need, and I know how to ask questions in a way that will stand up in court."

Heather dropper her gaze. "I'm sorry," she said. "I didn't mean to compromise anything."

Ryan's finger beneath her chin raised her eyes back to his. "The most important reason I don't want you involved is because I don't want you to get hurt," he said. "It's not court; it's you. I don't want the murderer to come after you, too."

***

So how was your date last night? Heather texted Amy. Did you get your hair done?

But instead of pinging with an incoming text, the phone began to play "Here Comes the Sun." Heather picked it up. "Hello?"

"No, I did not get my hair done before the date, and it's a good thing," Amy said. "Otherwise, Chris would have run away and never looked back."

"What do you mean?" Heather asked. She chose a spot in the parking lot of Wal-Mart, pulled in, and put the car in park so she could sit and finish the conversation.

"I mean that I got my hair done this morning," Amy said. "Your girl wasn't available, so I picked another salon. Nice looking little place in a building full of boutique-y type shops." She paused, and then said dramatically, "Now, I'm ready to be Medusa for Halloween. No, wait. I don't have that much hair left. Maybe Demi Moore. In her bald phase."

"It can't be that bad, can it?" Heather asked hopefully.

"Come see it," Amy said. "I'm at home. I'll be staying here until my hair grows out enough that I can get it cut right and show my face in public again."

The line went dead, and Heather looked at the screen. Amy had hung up.

There was only one thing a best friend could do. Wal-Mart would have to wait. Heather backed out of the space and drove toward the exit.

***

"Come in!" Amy shouted.

Heather turned the knob, opened the door, and let herself into Amy's house. But she didn't see any sign of her friend. "Amy, where are you?" she called out.

"I'm hiding," Amy said. "Now promise me you won't laugh or make jokes."

"Okay," Heather said, stopping in the middle of Amy's living room. "I won't laugh or make jokes, no matter how bad it is, scout's honor."

Slowly, Amy stepped around the corner from the hallway into the living room. She wore jeans and a t-shirt. Her light brown hair was cut in a short shag, the ends curled up and away from her face. Heather's mouth dropped open.

"Is it that bad?" Amy asked, raising a hand to her head. She sounded perilously close to tears.

"Bad?" Heather squeaked. "Are you kidding? You look gorgeous!"

"You can tell me the truth," Amy sniffled. "I can take it."

"The truth is that you look gorgeous," Heather repeated. "How can you not like that haircut on you?"

"Because it's so short," Amy said. "I've never had it this short. Ever. She must have cut off 6 inches."

"It's adorable," Heather insisted. "Look how it frames your face. It really makes your eyes look lovely, too. I wish I could do that to my hair."

"You do?" Amy said, her voice sounding slightly stronger.

"Yes, I do," Heather said. She grabbed Amy's arm and led her down the hall to the bathroom, shoving her in front of the mirror. "Just look at yourself. Most women would kill to look like you."

"But it's all spiky on the ends."

"It's not spiky, it's just turned up. That's the way it's supposed to be. You're gorgeous, girlfriend. So it's shorter than what you're used to. But it's perfect. I guess it is a good thing you didn't have your new 'do before you went out with Chris last night. He wouldn't have been able to keep his hands off you."

"That might have been okay," Amy said, the first hint of a smile turning up the corners of her mouth. She glanced sideways at Heather. "He did kiss me, though."

"Of course, he did," Heather said. "You're an amazing woman. You're sweet, and funny, and talented, and kind. And you're beautiful. You were beautiful then, and your hair looks even more amazing now."

"Well…maybe it does," Amy hedged as she peered into the mirror. "I guess it'll just take some getting used to."

"When you're used to it, you'll love it," Heather promised.

"Maybe." Amy's voice sounded like she might actually believe it. "Thanks for coming over to cheer me up."

"What are friends for?" she said.

"So what's the latest about Kelly?" Amy asked as they headed back to the living room.

"Not much," Heather answered. "All I know is that there were some kids arrested nearby the night she was killed. They had some pot and a gun."

"Potheads don't usually go around killing people," Amy said.

"Yeah, I know. But she had to be bludgeoned with something. Maybe it was their gun. Maybe they were trying to rob her."

"If you say so."

"Oh, and do you know Lana Sturmer?"

"No. Who's that?"

"Apparently a very arrogant diva type who always brought her daughter Emily in to have Kelly do her hair before the beauty pageants she competed in. Some of the competitions, Emily won, and everything was fine. But the last pageant she competed in, she came in runner-up. Lana came back to complain to Kelly. Started yelling at her in front of other customers. Said it was Kelly's fault Emily hadn't won."

Amy rolled her eyes. "Whatever. I can't stand people like that."

"Me either. Anyway, it sounds like every potential suspect the police have is a kid or has something to do with the high school."

"In that case, add one more name to your list," Amy said.

"What do you mean?"

"Brent Riggleman. He and Kelly had a bad break-up not that long before she died."

"Brent and Kelly were dating?"

"Well, not exactly," Amy said. "That was part of the problem. He wanted them to date; she didn't."

"Do you think Brent would have killed her over it?"

"Who knows?" Amy led the way into her living room and flopped down on the couch. "It's always those quiet, bitter types you have to worry about."

"Was he bitter?" Heather asked, just as she remembered Ryan's words only hours ago. "Wait. Never mind. Don't tell me, tell Ryan."

"Tell Ryan? Why would I do that?"

"Because if it looks like I'm running my own investigation, a good defense attorney could raise all kind of issues."

"But I'm your best friend. Can't we talk?"

"We can talk, but in terms of information that has to do with a murder investigation, I have to refer you to Ryan," Heather said.

"Well, okay," Amy said, squinting at her. "Did Ryan read you the riot act today or something?"

"Not exactly. He just told me what's best. And he said that his ultimate concern is not what happens in court, but what might happen to me. He doesn't want the murderer to come after me, too."

"I suppose he's got a point there."

"Yeah, it's a bummer. But I understand."

"Anything for the man you love, right?"

"Something like that," Heather said, unable to hide either her smile or the blush creeping into her cheeks.

***

After snarfing down a sandwich and some chips for supper with Amy, then making her Wal-Mart run, Heather finally headed home. Coming in through the back door as she usually did, she thought she heard the faint sound of the front doorbell.

She dropped her purse on the counter and walked swiftly through the kitchen and living room to the front door. Glancing through the peephole, the only thing she could see was a bouquet of flowers.

"Hi there," she said, opening the door to let Ryan in.

But it wasn't Ryan. The person who had rung her doorbell wore a polo shirt and khakis. A van parked at the curb behind him bore a decal along the side that read McKinley Florist. "Flowers for Heather Janke?" he said.

"I'm Heather," she said. The deliveryman held the vase of roses toward her, and she accepted it.

"There's a card," the man said, pointing. "Enjoy your flowers. Have a nice day."

"You too," Heather said. Smiling, she shut the door behind him, then set the flowers on the coffee table and plucked the small, white envelope from the plastic pitchfork-looking holder.

Opening the envelope and sliding out the card written in Ryan's hand, she read, Tomorrow's my turn to cook. See you at my place at 7:00? A heart was the only signature.

Heather retrieved her cell phone from her purse on the kitchen counter and texted back, "See you then. The flowers are beautiful. Thank you."

Chapter 5

"The Cinnamon Crumble donuts are a big hit," Maricela said as Heather stepped into the kitchen of Donut Delights. "Angelica's making some more right now."

Angelica glanced Heather's way, smiled, then turned back to her work of coating the tops of the donuts with pecan crumbles and the butter-brown sugar-cinnamon glaze.

"Great!" Heather said. "You never know how a new donut's going to go over."

"Seriously?" Maricela asked. "Have you ever had a flop?"

"Once," Heather said. She shuddered. "Let's not even talk about it."

"Well, this one seems to be pretty popular," Maricela said. "I'd say it's going over just fine."

"Good," Heather said.

As she began stuffing her hair into a hairnet, a strident female voice called out from the front counter, "Excuse me? Miss?"

Heather glanced over to see a middle-aged woman holding a half-eaten donut out in front of her as if it were poison. She put on her best professional smile and approached the counter.

"Yes, ma'am? May I help you?"

"This donut is awful," the woman said. She set it down on top of the glass case and jerked her hand away. "What's in it?"

"That's one of our new Cinnamon Crumble donuts," Heather said.

"It's a cinnamon-flavored donut with pecan crumble topping, coated with a special glaze made of butter, cinnamon, and brown sugar."

"Well I don't care what's in it," the customer said. "It's awful. I can't believe how much you charged me for this—this—"

"If you'd like, you can try another donut," Heather said. "On the house. Any variety you'd like."

"I don't want another donut." The woman grimaced. "It would probably be as bad as this one."

"Then I'd be happy to refund your money. Was there anything else that wasn't to your satisfaction?"

"The coffee wasn't very good, either," she said. "But I managed to drink it."

"Ma'am, I'll be glad to refund your money for the coffee, too," Heather said, moving toward the register.

"Well, you should. It's the least you can do."

Heather rang up the price of a donut and a cup of coffee, counted out the woman's refund, and handed it to her.

"And I won't be coming back," she said. "The prices you charge for these donuts! You should be ashamed of yourself."

Heather kept her smile pasted to her face until the customer had gathered up her purse and left the store. Then, she turned back towards the kitchen, drew in a deep breath, and let it out slowly.

"You were so nice to her," Angelica said. "But she was very nasty toward you. Why would you be so nice to her?"

"Because she's a customer," Heather said.

"Not anymore."

"Then maybe just because it's the right thing to do."

"I glad she's not coming back. We don't need any costumers like her."

"For every one of her, there are 99 delightful ones," Heather said. "Gotta take the good with the bad sometimes."

"You're the boss," Angelica muttered as she turned back to her work. "But I don't like the way they talk to you."

Heather smiled as she grabbed an apron, slipped the strap over her head, and tied it behind herself. Maybe you couldn't make everybody happy, she thought, because there was just no pleasing some people. But if you could spend most of your life making most people happy, as she had the privilege to do, then you had nothing to complain about. In fact, you were very blessed.

***

"Sorry," Amy said, giggling. "Hee hee. Sorry again."

The white-coated pedicurist working on Amy's right foot didn't look up. She was probably used to customers with ticklish feet, Heather figured.

As another pedicurist worked on Heather's foot, Heather leaned back against the leather chair and sighed. The constant, low hum of the vibrations as the chair massaged her back provided a soothing background noise that almost lulled her to sleep. That, and the fact that the foot not being worked on rested in a tub of delightfully warm water.

"Ahhhh," Heather sighed. "I could really get used to this."

"You should get a mani-pedi more often," Amy said. "Hee hee. Because you're on your feet all day. Ha! Sorry. Maybe I better not try to talk to you until she's done with my feet."

"You're funny," Heather said. She closed her eyes. In a moment, she felt the pedicurist gently place her foot back into the warm water, then lift her other foot to be worked on. "I just don't pamper myself very often," she said to Amy. "You know?"

"Every woman needs pampering once in a while," Amy said,

sighing in relief as the woman placed her foot back into the water. "Preferably often."

"Mmm," Heather murmured noncommittally. Once in awhile was fine with her, but pampering herself too often would feel...decadent, maybe. Or wasteful, in terms of money.

"I know what you're thinking," Amy said.

"What am I thinking?"

"That it costs too much. That it's too indulgent. Something like that."

"Right-o."

"Okay, then," Amy said. "Marry Ryan and let him pamper you."

"He hasn't asked," Heather said.

"Would you marry him if he did?"

"You want the same color polish on your toes as on your fingers?" The nail tech was looking up at Heather, saving her from having to answer Amy's question.

"Yes, please," she said gratefully.

It wasn't that she hadn't thought about it, or that she didn't know the answer. The answer was an unqualified, resounding yes. Yes, she would marry Ryan if he asked.

So why didn't she want to admit that to her best friend?

Throughout the rest of the pedicure, as the nail tech finished up and then eased the thin, foam flip-flops onto Heather's feet, she pondered the reason. And as she and Amy sat at the ultraviolet station after their manicures, their hands resting on the counter, fingers spread apart under the rays, the answer finally came to her.

Other than herself, she wanted Ryan to be the first person to whom she would ever acknowledge her desire to marry him.

That is, if he ever asked.

***

"So what do you have planned for this evening?" Amy asked, spooning a huge bite of sprinkle-covered frozen yogurt into her mouth.

"Ryan's going to cook dinner," Heather said. As a mother with two toddlers in tow eased past their table in the food court, Heather reached down and scooted her bags closer to her feet.

"Ooooh, a man who cooks!" Amy said.

"I assume he does. He's never really cooked for me before. But the other day, when I cooked dinner for him, he claimed to be a—in his words—'great' cook."

"So what's he making you?"

"I don't know. The card just invited me to dinner at 7:00 at his place."

"Card? What card?"

"The one in the bouquet of roses," Heather answered.

"Roses? An entire dozen?"

Heather nodded.

"What color?"

"Red."

"You got a dozen red roses, and you didn't tell me? Your best friend?" Amy placed a hand to her chest, feigning hurt feelings.

"I guess I just didn't think of it," Heather said.

"Whatever. Okay, so you definitely need to wear that maxi dress you bought tonight. Red roses are for passion, so he's obviously attracted to you. As if we didn't both know that. So it wouldn't hurt to fan the flames a little bit."

"I was planning on wearing it," Heather said, taking a bite of her own sundae, and then deliberately changing the subject. "So when's your next date with Chris?"

"It may or may not be tonight," Amy said. Then she leaned in closer and said in a stage whisper, "Why do you think I bought that little mini-dress?"

Heather laughed. She stopped when she saw Amy staring toward the other side of the food court. "What?" she asked. "What's wrong?"

"Don't look now," Amy said, "but there's Brent Riggleman sitting over there by Orange Julius."

So of course, Heather looked. "Oh, I see him," she said. "Hmm. He's by himself."

"He's kind of a loner," Amy said. "Hadn't really dated anybody for awhile until he got interested in Kelly."

"Have you told all this to Ryan?" Heather asked, trying not to stare at Brent, who sat eating a piece of cheesecake.

"Yep. He said thanks. But I don't think there's anything wrong with us talking about it. I don't have any actual information that you don't already know. Just speculation, conjecture and wild guesses."

"Brent has always seemed pleasant the few times I've run into him at an event or something."

"Yep, that's Brent. Always smiling. Unassuming. Meek. That's why you have to watch out for guys like him. You never know what they could be planning."

"Have you ever seen him angry?"

"Well, once," Amy said, her voice suddenly serious. "And before you ask, I told Ryan about this, too. I once saw Brent get pretty upset about a snide comment somebody made about him. I didn't think it was a big deal. But I guess Brent did." Amy paused. "That was the first and only time I ever saw him really, really angry."

"I wish I could go over there and talk to him," Heather said. "Just ask him a few questions."

"But Ryan wouldn't like it?"

"Nope. And I understand why not. I mean, I'm not a professional. He's right. And I see what a defense attorney could make out of my involvement. But it's killing me to sit here and not go talk to him."

"There's no reason I can't go talk to him," Amy said, spooning up the last bit of her fro-yo.

"No. Don't," Heather said.

"Why not? I'm not dating Ryan Shepherd. He didn't tell me to keep my little nosey nose out of this case."

"Please don't," Heather said. "I don't want him to think I'm trying to find a way to get around what he asked me to do. Or not do."

"Okay," Amy sighed. "Although I don't guess it would really do any good to talk to him, anyway. I mean, what, we say, 'So, Brent, you seem to be a mild-mannered guy, but I bet you really get angry sometimes. Were you angry that Kelly wouldn't date you? How angry were you? Oh, and by the way, did you kill her?'"

"Yeah, probably not," she agreed. "That kind of confession only happens on TV."

"Perry Mason," Amy said. "That's how it always went. Perry would get the killer up on the witness stand, and everybody knew it was the killer, but the guy just hadn't confessed yet. And somehow, Perry always got them to give themselves up."

"Oooh, and like in A Few Good Men, too," Heather added. "Where Tom Cruise provokes Jack Nicholson into admitting that he ordered the code red."

"I haven't seen that movie," Amy said.

"You what? Never? How did I not know this? You have lived a sheltered and deprived life, girlfriend."

"Is it a romance?"

"No. There actually isn't any romance involved. For once."

"Then what's the point of the movie?"

"Only truth triumphing over lies," Heather said. "Good triumphing over evil. Right overcoming wrong."

"Too bad real life doesn't work like that," Amy said.

"Sometimes it does. Sometimes things turn out right."

"Think that'll happen in Kelly's murder?" Amy stared across the food court at Brent as he threw his trash in the trashcan and set his tray on top.

"I hope so," Heather said.

"Because she was a good person, you know?" Amy said.

"Not just a good hairdresser, but a truly good person. And she didn't deserve what happened to her. No matter who did it. Or why."

Chapter 6

When she got home, Heather let Dave out and walked down the hall to her room, still holding her shopping bags. She set them on her bed and began pulling things from them one by one. The deep burgundy maxi dress was, with its silver accents around the hem, was, in her opinion, just perfect for her medium-red hair, fair skin, and green eyes.

She was well aware that some people believed redheads shouldn't wear red, but in her opinion, you just had to choose the right red to complement your own coloring.

Next, she drew a shoebox out of another bag. The silver sandals, she set on the bed next to the dress. At the mall, she'd debated whether or not she should buy them, but now, she was glad she had. They were chic but not too fancy—which was good, since "fancy" had never been her style. She much preferred simple and elegant.

The chunky silver bracelet and silver hoop earrings, she laid on the top of her dresser. Then, she went into her tiny bathroom with its clawfoot tub to run a bath. She turned on the hot water, waited for it to heat up, then turned on the cold to lower the temperature to just below steaming.

While she waited for the tub to fill, she twisted her hair up on top of her head and clipped it in place. Then she let her clothes fall into a heap on the floor and slipped into the nearly-steaming water.

This was the kind of pampering she enjoyed—a nice, hot bath when she didn't really need one because she'd taken a shower that morning. Time to soak up the heat, lean her head back and just be.

Of course, she couldn't be for too long; she wanted to have plenty of time to get ready for her date with Ryan. That was another luxury she enjoyed—taking her time getting dressed and accessorizing, then attempting to do something with her sometimes contrary tresses.

Heather stuck her feet up out of the water and wiggled her toes. She'd chosen clear nail polish, instead of a more prominent color such as burgundy. There was such a thing as one's ensemble being too coordinated.

When her fingers began to look like prunes, she reluctantly got out of the tub. Drying off, she wrapped the towel around her and headed for the bedroom just as her cell phone started ringing.

Ryan. "Hello?" she said.

"Hey, Beautiful," Ryan said. " Are you getting ready to head over here?"

"In about twenty minutes," she said.

"Great. Are you hungry?"

"Starved," she said.

"So, twenty minutes? Not ten, not thirty?"

"I'll be there at seven, on he dot" she said.

"Perfect. See you then." The line went dead.

Heather frowned quizzically at the phone, and then smiled. Glancing at the clock on her nightstand, she saw that it was 6:29. Time to get dressed.

***

Thirty-one minutes later, at exactly 7:00, Heather stood on Ryan's front porch ringing the doorbell. He answered the door in slacks and a white dress shirt. Standing aside, he invited her in with a sweep of his arm. "This way, Madame," he said.

"Merci, monsieur," Heather replied, dredging up one of the few French phrases she knew.

"May I take your purse?"

"But of course." Heather handed it to him, and he placed it on the coffee table.

"It smells wonderful in here," she said, sniffing the mouth-watering aromas emanating from the kitchen.

"Your table waits," Ryan said. "And may I say that Madame looks beautiful?"

"Of course you may," Heather said, smiling.

He led her to the kitchen table, where he held her chair for her as she sat down. Before her was a salad plate laden with greens artfully dressed. One goblet at her place held water; the other wine. Heather took one look at the presentation and realized that she had grossly underestimated him.

She said nothing until he sat down across from her. "This looks fantastic," she said. "Thank you. Already."

"You ain't seen nothin' yet," Ryan said, dropping the formality and grinning in that way she knew and loved. "Just wait til the main course."

Heather took a bite of her salad. "Mmm, this dressing is delicious," she said. "What kind is it?"

"I made it," Ryan said simply.

"You made it? Like, from various oils and spices and things?"

"Yep."

"Wow. Um, okay. I'm kind of feeling bad for serving you Wish-Bone dressing."

"I love to cook," Ryan said. "You don't. Yet you made a delicious meal anyway. I'd call that a win."

She took another bite of salad. "You're not on call tonight, are you?"

"Nope. Bill's catching. Tonight, I'm all yours."

"Promise?" Heather asked, arching her eyebrows at him.

"Don't make me prove it," Ryan said, "or we'll never get to the main course." He pushed back his chair and stood. "Be right back," he said.

She saw him open the oven door and peer inside. "I believe our main course is ready," he announced. Wearing one oven mitt, he deftly removed the pan from the oven. On it sat two steaks that looked absolutely luscious even from several feet away.

Heather watched him check the temperature, then place each one on a dinner plate. He removed the lid from a pan on the stovetop and spooned something on top of each steak. Finally, he added a slice of French bread to each plate, and then set hers in front of her with a flourish.

Sautéed mushrooms topped the meat, the wine sauce in which they had been marinated mingling with the juices from the steak. "Wow," she said as Ryan took his seat. "I can't wait to taste this."

"Dig in," he said. "Let me know if it's cooked the way you like it."

As she sliced off a bite of steak, she could see just a hint of pink. "Perfect," she said. She raised the fork to her mouth and let the meat settle on her tongue. As she began to chew and the rich savoriness of the combined flavors filled her mouth, she rolled her eyes heavenward. "This is so good," she said. "I can never cook for you again. Nothing I make is anywhere near this good."

"Should everyone in the world stop painting because they're not Monet?" he asked. "What about all the Renoirs and Van Goghs? The world needs their art, too. It would be a tragedy if they stopped painting because they couldn't paint water lilies like Monet could."

"Point taken," she said. "So what else don't I know about you? What other surprises will I find out along the way?"

"None that I know of," he said. "What you see is what you get. I'm just a guy with a cat and a taste for beer who happens to solve mysteries for a living."

"Don't sell yourself short," she said. "You're not 'just' an anything. You're an amazing guy who makes justice triumph for a living, and who also happens to be a gourmet chef and look pretty darn good even in jeans and a t-shirt."

"So, about that cop thing," Ryan said, cutting another bite of his steak. "You don't mind dating a cop? You don't mind it when I get called away from a date, or when I have to go to work instead of spending time with you?"

"I don't like it," Heather said. "But I don't resent it. I know its part of your job. It's what you do. I knew that before we started dating. And I admire you for it."

"Really?" Ryan's dark eyes were on hers.

"Really," she said. "I'm proud of you and what you do. I'm proud that you're one of the good guys. That what you do, matters. That you're good at it. That people like you are the reason people like me can sleep peacefully at night. Yes, I'd like to have more time together sometimes. But I wouldn't wish away anything about you. It's part of what makes you who you are."

Ryan's gaze dropped to his plate as he nodded. He busied himself cutting another bite of steak as he cleared his throat. It seemed like forever before he met her gaze once more.

"Favorite sports team?" he asked, raising one eyebrow.

"Uh, I don't really have one."

"You don't? How can you not have a favorite sports team?"

"The same way you probably don't have a favorite interior decorator," she said.

"Hey, women can like sports, too. And guys can decorate their homes. Look at my house." He spread his arms wide, inviting her to take it all in. "I have my very own style. I call it 'Bachelor Chic.'"

She laughed. "It works," she said, pushing her plate away. "Ugh, I'm stuffed. The steak was so delicious I ate too much. I may never eat again."

"Not even if I made a dessert?" Ryan asked.

Heather groaned. "What is it?"

"Cheesecake," he said smugly. "With homemade cherry topping."

"I could not possibly fit a slice of cheesecake in on top of all this," she said, patting her flat stomach.

"I'm too full. Could we save it for later?"

"Of course," he said. "Madame's wish is my command."

When Ryan rose to begin clearing the table, Heather piled her own silverware on top of her plate. "I can get it," he said. "You take your glass of wine to the den and have a seat."

"Gladly," she agreed with a smile. She settled in on Ryan's sofa and waited, sipping her wine and listening to the sounds coming from the kitchen as he cleared the table and put the dishes in the sink.

In another minute, he sat down on the couch next to her. "I've really enjoyed tonight," he said.

"Me too." Heather put her glass of wine on the coffee table and turned to face him. "Thank you for that incredible meal."

"I enjoyed cooking for you," Ryan said. He hesitated, holding her gaze with his. Then he said his voice husky, "In fact, if it were possible, I'd cook for you every night of our lives."

Heather felt the trembling start in the very center of her body and found herself utterly unable to speak.

"You said earlier that you don't mind dating a cop," he said. "Do you think you'd want to be married to one?"

Heather's hand seemed to rise and cover her mouth of its own volition as tears sprang to her eyes. Slowly, never taking his eyes off hers, Ryan knelt before her on one knee and reached for her hands. "Heather, I've never known anyone like you," he said.

"You're smart, you're funny, and you're amazing. You're beautiful. I want to go to sleep by your side every night and wake up next to you every morning."

He stopped to clear his throat, and Heather realized with amazement that there were tears in his eyes, too. "Heather, I love you," he said, his voice cracking.

"I know I don't deserve you, but you would make me the happiest man in the world if you would agree to be my wife. Heather, will you marry me?"

Her tears spilled over, and she reached for him blindly, feeling his strong arms go around her.

"Yes," she murmured against his cheek through her tears. "Yes, I'll become the happiest woman in the world and marry you."

His lips found hers, and he kissed her, deeply and passionately. Then he pulled away and fumbled in his pocket. He drew out a small, black velvet box and opened it to display the ring she knew she would wear for the rest of her life—a square-cut, sparkling diamond solitaire. She held out a trembling hand as he placed it on her ring finger. It fit like it had been made for her, and maybe it had. How he had known her ring size, she didn't know. But she figured if he could figure out who killed whom, of course he'd be able to determine what size ring she wore.

"You pick out the wedding band," he said. "Anything you want, and it's yours."

Staring at the ring on her finger, Heather tilted her hand this way and that, watching the light play off the brilliance of the diamond. "I can't believe this," she said with a laugh. "We're really going to get married."

"Yes, we really are," Ryan said. "And the sooner, the better. Take all the time you want to make plans. Just don't take too long. In fact, let's get married right now. I could call a friend, who just happens to be a Justice of the Peace."

At the hopeful, little-boy look on his face, Heather laughed out loud and threw her arms around him. "I love you so much," she just had time to say before his lips found hers again.

***

Later that night, just before she finally went to sleep in her own bed, Heather picked up her phone. Navigating her way through her favorite app, she selected a new ringtone to use as her default ringtone.

"Here Comes the Sun" had served her well for awhile. But it was time for a change. Now, if someone called her, her phone would play "Here Comes the Bride."

Heather set her phone to "silent," turned off the bedside lamp, and snuggled beneath the covers, a smile on her face.

Chapter 7

The next morning at 8:30, tired but still ecstatic, Heather entered the kitchen of Donut Delights. Somehow, despite her excitement, she'd fallen asleep last night. But it had taken awhile. As a result, she'd actually slept until the alarm woke her up.

"Good morning," Angelica greeted her. "Hey! What is that on your hand?" She crossed the kitchen in three strides and seized Heather's left hand. "It's a ring! He finally asked you to marry him. You're getting married. Congratulations." She threw her arms around Heather in a bear hug.

Almost before Heather knew it, they were all hugging: she, Angelica, Maricela, Jung, and Ken. "Congratulations!" Maricela said. "It's about time!"

They all laughed. "I still can't believe it!" Heather said.

"When did this happen?"

"Last night."

"So tell us all about it. How did he propose? What did he say?"

"Well, he invited me to dinner, which he cooked himself,"

Heather said. "Salad with the best dressing I've ever tasted, steak with a white wine mushroom sauce, and French bread. He proposed after dinner. He said I would make him the happiest man in the world if I would marry him."

"He cooks and he's romantic," Angelica said. "He's perfect for you."

"Thanks, everybody," Heather said.

"So when's the wedding?"

"We haven't set a date yet," she said. "But you guys will be among the first to know. You all have to be there."

"Of course we'll be there," Angelica said. "We will sit in the front row and cry how beautiful you are. Boo-hoo!" She rubbed her eyes, pretending to cry.

Again, they laughed. "Much as I'd love to talk about this all day long," Heather said, "I guess we'd better get to work."

A female customer stood waiting rather impatiently at the front counter. Heather grabbed a hair net and stuffed her hair into it as she walked up front. "Good morning. May I help you?"

Despite the woman's perfect makeup, she looked tired. "I need a dozen Southern Pecan Pie donuts and a dozen Ice Cream Sundae donuts," she said abruptly.

"Yes, ma'am," Heather said, grabbing a flat, white cardboard box from beneath the counter and assembling it by popping the sides up and locking the tabs in place.

"And don't just smash them together," the woman added. "I want them to look nice when I get where I'm going."

"Yes, ma'am," Heather said again, noticing that the artfully applied makeup was actually concealing bags under the woman's eyes. Maybe she was cranky because she was so tired.

Heather finished with the first box of donuts and placed it on the counter in front of the customer. As she reached for a second box to assemble, she saw the woman try unsuccessfully to stifle a yawn. "Long day?" Heather said politely.

"Not that it's any of your business, but no," the woman said. "It's the pageant circuit. Competing in beauty pageants is exhausting."

Heather tried not to let her surprise show on her face. The woman looked to be in her early 40's. As far as Heather knew, there weren't a whole slew of beauty pageants for 40-year-old women.

"Fortunately," her customer continued, "Emily wins every pageant she enters."

Wait a minute, Heather thought. Her daughter's name was Emily? Was this woman Lana Sturmer?

"Congratulations to Emily," Heather said. "She must be beautiful."

"She is," the woman said. "It was too bad that stupid hairdresser messed up her hair right before the Miss Harper County pageant. Otherwise, she would have won that one, too."

"She didn't win?" Heather asked, beginning to place donuts in the second box.

"She was runner-up."

"That's great."

"First runner-up is still first loser. That—that woman—deserved what she got."

"You mean the hairdresser who was murdered recently?" Heather asked innocently.

"Yes. The once who was bludgeoned to death with her own flat iron."

"Wow. I didn't know those things were heavy enough to kill somebody with."

"Apparently so. At least, that's what the paper said."

"Hmm. Well, that's too bad."

"If you say so," the woman said with a sniff.

Yep, Heather thought. That has to be Lana Sturmer. Who else in town has both a daughter who wins beauty pageants and an attitude like that?

She finished preparing Lana's order and rang it up at the register. When she announced the total, Lana pulled cash from her purse and thrust it at Heather. She snatched the change Heather handed her, stuffed it in her wallet, grabbed the boxes of donuts, and stalked toward the door.

"Whew," Heather said as the door closed behind her.

"Who in the world was that?" Maricela asked.

"Lana Sturmer," Heather said. "Excuse me a minute. I have to text Ryan and tell him I talked to her."

She hurried into her office, retrieved her phone from her purse in the bottom desk drawer, and rattled off a quick text. I just met Lana Sturmer. I think. She came into the shop and ordered donuts. She brought up the murder. But I didn't ask her any questions. Just thought you should know.

She laid the phone on her desk, leaned back in her chair, and swiveled it back and forth, waiting for his return text. It arrived a couple minutes later. Thanks, babe. Hey, did I tell you that you looked beautiful last night?

Heather smiled. You might have, she texted. But you can always tell me again.

You looked beautiful, he answered. Love you.

Love you too. She hit "send," dropped her phone back into her purse, and returned to the kitchen, still smiling.

***

"Ooh, what do you think of this one?" Amy pointed to the picture on the right-hand page.

"Too low-cut," Heather said. What was with wedding gowns these days, anyway?

"Girl, it doesn't hurt to show a little cleavage," Amy said.

"Cleavage? At a wedding?"

"Okay, maybe not," Amy said, flipping the page in the bridal magazine. "How about this one?"

"Too frilly," she said. "I don't want to look like it's my quinceañera. It's my wedding. My second wedding, no less."

"That doesn't mean you can't look stylish."

"And who gets to decide what's stylish? Some of these are just plain ugly."

"True," Amy conceded. "So let's find you one that's stylish in a way that you like. And in a way that flatters your gorgeous figure."

"What gorgeous figure?"

"Yours, girlfriend," Amy said. "Give yourself some credit, huh?"

She flipped another page. "Oh, now here's one. This one would look fantastic on you."

"Wow," Heather breathed. "That's gorgeous." The sheath dress had an asymmetrical neckline with a wide band at the waist. Sheer fabric rose from the top of the band to gather over one shoulder and flow down the model's back to the floor, even longer than the dress's short train.

"Think this might be the one?" Amy asked.

"Maybe so," Heather said in awe.

Amy folded down the upper corner of the page. "We'll come back to this one," she said. "So are you going to get your dress heirloomed?"

"I don't know. I hadn't thought that far ahead. Probably so."

"You have to think about stuff like that. Do you know yet how much time you have to think about it?"

"We haven't set a date yet, if that's what you're asking," Heather said. "But we're thinking sometime around New Year's."

"That's only two and a half months away," Amy said, fixing her with a stern glance. "You do realize that, right?"

"Why wait?" Heather protested. "It's not like this is a first wedding for either of us. It won't be as big and fancy as the first time around. Simple, yet elegant. That's what I'm going for."

"What about Ryan? What does he want?"

"Ryan just wants to get married," she said. "He'd just run down to the Justice of the Peace if I would go for that."

"But you won't," Amy said firmly. "That's totally not romantic. And second wedding or not, you want a wedding to remember."

"I'd remember the Justice of the Peace," Heather teased.

"Yeah, but not in a good way."

"True."

"So if this really is the dress, you've gotten the second most important part out of the way," Amy said.

"The first most important part being finding a groom?" Heather asked.

"You got it," Amy said.

***

Long after Amy had left, leaving the stack of bridal magazines piled on Heather's coffee table, Heather sat on the couch flipping through their glossy pages. Every now and then, she folded down a page corner to mark a dress she wanted to come back to and look at a second time.

But her thoughts weren't entirely on what she was seeing. Finally, she gave up, laid the open magazine down on the coffee table, and turned her attention to trying to figure out what was bothering her.

Something kept stirring at the back of her mind, some thought or idea that wouldn't quite come into focus. What was it?

Starting with getting up that morning, Heather mentally reviewed the events of her day. As she worked forward toward arriving at Donut Delights, the nagging feeling got stronger. When she got to her encounter with Lana Sturmer, alarm bells began going off. Why?

Lana had looked pretty tired that morning. Her unpleasant attitude might have had no more significance than that. But wait...

Heather sat up straight as the idea began to come into focus. Lana had said she was tired because the pageant circuit was exhausting. But hadn't the Miss Harper County pageant been over for several days? Shouldn't she have had time to relax by now?

On the other hand, maybe Emily was preparing for an upcoming pageant. Maybe that's what Lana had meant.

But that possibility didn't feel right. Heather thought about googling pageants in the area but realized that would probably come too close to Ryan's definition of getting involved in the investigation. Instead, she texted him, "Hi, handsome. Please call me when you get a chance. I have an idea you might want to check out if you haven't already."

But even though she waited several minutes, no ping

announced a response from Ryan.

She'd been sitting long enough, first looking at magazines with Amy, then continuing to peruse them on her own. She didn't feel like sitting around waiting for Ryan to call. He'd call as soon as he could. She might as well find something to do in the meantime.

"Hey, Dave," she called to her dog, who was sleeping on his doggie bed in the corner. Dave lifted his head and blinked at her. "You want to go for a walk?"

At the word 'walk,' Dave lumbered to his feet, shook

himself all over, and trotted eagerly to the back door. "Sure, you know what that means," Heather said, lifting his leash off the hook by the door and clipping it to his collar. She stuck her cell phone in her pocket and grabbed her keys from her purse on the counter. "Okay, let's go."

As Dave led her enthusiastically down the steps, she felt a twinge of guilt for not taking him on walks more often. It was just so much easier to let him out in the back yard to do his business. It was a big yard, and if he wanted to run around and play while he was out there, he had plenty of room.

"Maybe we'll start going on more walks anyway," Heather told him, as if he'd been privy to her thoughts. "Although winter's coming, so who knows?"

They followed the driveway to the sidewalk, then turned right and walked to the corner. Turning right again, they passed the front of Heather's house and continued down the block.

It was dusk, and Heather knew they didn't have much time before the sun would go down completely. Well, maybe just a short walk this time. Next time, they could go longer.

Her cell phone vibrated, then began to play the Wedding March. Heather wondered if she would ever get tired of hearing that song. "Hang on just a second, Dave," she said, stopping to fish the phone out of her pocket.

Dave didn't mind. He found an interesting tree nearby and marked his territory while she answered the phone. "Hello?"

"Hey, Beautiful, it's me. I got your text. What did you want me to check out?"

"Well, you know how I was talking to Lana Sturmer this morning?"

"Yeah."

Dave finished his business and tugged on the leash as he started forward. Heather followed him.

"Well, I was just thinking. She said she was tired because the pageant circuit was so exhausting. But the last pageant Emily competed in was several days ago. She should have had time to rest by now, if that was the problem."

"Maybe Emily's preparing for an upcoming pageant," Ryan said.

"That's what I was thinking. So I was wondering if you knew if there were any pageants coming up in this area anytime soon."

"I don't know," he said. "But I can look."

"Thanks," she said.

"No problem. So what did you think of Ms. Sturmer?"

"Lisa was right. Lana has an attitude. Imperious. I think that would be the word for it. And she's cold, too. She made some comment about how Kelly got what she deserved for messing up Emily's hair."

"What exactly did she say?" Ryan asked.

"Something like, 'That woman deserved what she got.' And I said something like, 'You mean the one who was murdered?' And she said, 'Yeah, the one who got bludgeoned to death with her own flat iron. And then—"

"What did she say?" Ryan's voice was suddenly tense. Excited.

"That Kelly deserved what she got?" Heather asked.

"No! The part after that."

"About how Kelly was bludgeoned with her own flat iron?"

"Heather, where are you?" Ryan demanded, his words spilling over each other. "Are you at home?"

"No, I'm out walking Dave," she said. "Ryan, what's going on? What's the big deal?"

"Lana Sturmer shouldn't have known that the murder weapon was a flat iron," Ryan said.

"Apparently she reads the paper. She said the paper said it was a flat iron."

"The paper never said that," Ryan said, his voice intense. "Heather, how far are you from home?"

"Couple blocks. But Ryan, she said it was in the paper. She must have read it."

"I'm telling you it wasn't in the paper," Ryan insisted. "The murder weapon was the one detail we were keeping back from the media. I checked every inch of that paper every day to make sure it hadn't leaked."

Heather felt a cold chill creeping over her. "What are you saying?" she asked, already knowing the answer.

In the distance, a dark-colored car rounded the corner and drove slowly up the block in her direction.

"I'm saying there's no way she could have known about the murder weapon unless she was the one who killed Kelly. And if she ever finds out that the flat iron wasn't actually mentioned in the paper, she could come after you."

"What do I do?" Heather asked.

But his answer was drowned out in a squeal of tires. Whirling toward the sound, she could see nothing but the headlights blinding her as the dark car jumped the curb and sped straight toward her.

Heather screamed and threw herself to the side.

Chapter 8

She landed hard; the breath knocked out of her, she scrambled to her hands and knees, terror flooding every inch of her body. But the car had already swerved back into the street, tires spinning out smoke as it gained traction and fled. Heather dropped her head, staring at the grass as she fought to get her breath back.

Dave. Where was Dave?

She spotted him ten feet away, his furry white body lying in a crumpled heap. Dave!

Sobbing, she crawled toward him. With one hand, she stroked the fur of his lifeless body; with the other, she caressed his head.

And felt him lick her hand.

"Dave?" she managed through her tears. "Dave, are you okay?"

But he wasn't. He whined pitifully, just once, his limpid brown eyes looking up at her.

As gently as she could, Heather slid her hands beneath him. Again he whined, longer this time, and she knew she was hurting him. "I'm sorry, Dave," she said, trying to soothe him with her voice, as the sound of sirens in the distance grew louder and closer.

An ambulance? They were sending an ambulance for Dave?

No, of course not, she realized, cradling Dave's broken body in her arms as best she could and turning toward home. Nobody sent an ambulance for a dog, even one as beloved as hers. If there was an ambulance, it must be for her.

But more than likely, most of the sirens belonged to police vehicles. Gradually, her fear and grief was being replaced by another emotion. Lana Sturmer had tried to run her over. Tried to kill her! Fortunately, she was okay, except for a few bruises and scrapes that were beginning to make their presence felt. But Lana had almost killed Dave. And that made Heather very angry.

"Ma'am, are you okay?" The voice came from a man standing next to her. "Is your dog okay? Is this your cell phone?"

Heather had no idea who the man was, but it didn't matter. "I'm fine," she said, surprised that her voice sounded almost normal. "But my dog is hurt. I think he's hurt pretty badly."

"Do you want to take him to the emergency vet clinic on Highway 10?" the man asked.

"Yes. We were just out on a walk. I'm headed home to get my car."

"I live right there," he said, pointing to the house they were standing in front of. "I heard all the noise and came outside. If you want to wait right there, I'll go get my car and drive you to the vet."

The first police car zipped past them, and then screeched to a stop. An officer leaped out. "Ma'am?" he called. "Are you Heather?"

"Thank you so much," Heather said to the neighbor, "but I think help just arrived."

The next few minutes were a blur. Another patrol car arrived. And then, the person she'd most wanted to see. Ryan.

"Are you okay?" he asked her, looking deep into her eyes to see the truth for himself.

"Yes, I'm okay. But I need to get Dave to the emergency clinic."

"We'll take my car," he said. "It's right over there."

Right over there was the middle of the street. After speaking briefly to one of the patrol officers, Ryan walked beside her, with her carrying Dave as gently as she could. He held the door open for her as she got in, and then fastened the seat belt around her. Through it all, Dave was silent. He didn't move, except for periodically opening his eyes and looking up at Heather.

Ryan slid into his seat and buckled up. He maneuvered the car skillfully and smoothly through the tangle of vehicles in the street, and then took off.

In fifteen minutes, he braked to a stop in front of the clinic. A staff member in green scrubs held the door open for them. "His name is Dave," Ryan said. "He was hit by a car."

Within another few minutes, they had been shown into a small exam room. The vet swiftly determined the extent of Dave's injuries and recommended surgery. Heather agreed.

Almost before she knew it, she found herself sitting in a hard plastic chair in the waiting room next to Ryan, her head on his shoulder, his arm around her.

There must have been a thousand details Ryan had taken care of in order to handle the situation and make things easier for her, she knew. That was one thing she loved about him—his strength and his competence. Okay, make that two things.

The outside door opened, and a uniformed officer entered the waiting room. "Detective Shepherd?" he said, and Heather realized he must have been surprised to see Ryan's arm around her.

"This is my fiancée, Heather Janke," Ryan said. "Heather, we need you to answer some questions."

Heather nodded and sat up straight. "Ask me anything you want," she said. "I want to help you find her. She tried to kill me, and she almost killed my dog."

"Actually, ma'am, she's already been taken into custody," the officer said. "After she tried to hit you, she swerved back into the street and hit a parked car. A patrol unit saw a car turning onto Bowen with its front bumper half hanging off and initiated a traffic stop. Turned out it was the woman who tried to assault you."

"Thank you," Heather said. "Thank you for everything you guys have done."

"You're welcome, ma'am," the officer said. "There was an ambulance on scene near your residence. I have it on the way over here in case you would like them to check you out."

"No, thank you," Heather said. "I'm fine. Really. I'm angry, but I'm fine."

"Are you sure?"

"Yes, sir. Nothing a few band-aids and some rest won't cure. So go ahead. Ask me anything you want to know."

"Heather, I'm going to step outside," Ryan said. "This is a criminal case—not only the murder, but her attempt to kill you. I'm going to stay out of it as much as I can, but I'll be right outside. Okay?"

"Okay," she said. "I'll be fine. Just—don't go too far, okay?"

"You got it," Ryan said. He pushed through the same door through which the patrol officer had entered just moments before and went outside.

The officer sat down two chairs away from her and turned to face her. He withdrew a small notebook from a pocket in his uniform shirt and flipped it open. Clicking a ballpoint pen into readiness, he asked, "What is your full name, ma'am?"

***

Two hours later, Heather sat on her sofa snuggled against Ryan's side, their arms around each other. Dave's doggie bed was empty; the vet had recommended that he remain under observation at the clinic for 24 hours post-surgery.

"I'm glad they got her," Heather said.

Ryan didn't have to ask whom she was talking about. "Me, too. Both for Kelly's murder, and for the fact that she tried to kill you."

"I don't understand why she murdered Kelly," Heather said. "I know she did it, but why?"

"She's not talking," Ryan said. "The only thing she'll tell us is 'see my lawyer.' But if I had to guess, based on the evidence? I don't think she intended to kill her. I think she came back to the shop to continue the argument they started earlier. She got angry, grabbed the flat iron, and swung it in a fit of rage. The first blow probably knocked Kelly out. In any case, she fell to the floor. And Lana just kept swinging."

Heather shuddered. "Over hair, andnd coming in second place." She paused. "You know the person I feel sorry for in all this — besides Kelly— is Emily Sturmer. Lisa said she was a sweet kid.

She probably never wanted any of this."

"Probably not," Ryan agreed. For a moment, they sat in silence. "You know..." he said, leaning forward to pick up one of the bridal magazines that still lay on the table, "I just realized that I'm going to have to wear a tux for our wedding, aren't I?"

"You most certainly are," Heather said. "I'm the one who gets to wear the dress."

"You can have it," Ryan said. "I think I'll stick to the tux."

"Good plan," she said.

"But can I wear tennis shoes? Dress shoes can pinch."

"Not even once," Heather said. "You're going to look every inch the handsome guy I know and love. All my friends and relatives are going to be jealous."

"So are mine," Ryan said. "Listen, I know you have a lot of plans to make. But I want to set a date. I want to know exactly how much longer I have to wait before one of us doesn't have to go home at the end of the night. How does January 1 sound to you?"

"I think it sounds great," Heather said, smiling.

"I know it's not even three months. Will that give you enough time to get everything done?"

"Sure. If you'll help me."

"You actually want my help?"

"Well…maybe," Heather teased. "I'll let you know."

"You got it," Ryan said for the second time that night. "But can I make one suggestion?"

"Sure," she said.

"I think we need a ring bearer."

"Okay. Do you have somebody in mind?"

"Of course I do," he said, one corner of his mouth crooking upward in a grin. "I think it should be Dave."

"Dave?" she said. "You want a dog in our wedding?"

"Bella could be the flower girl."

"We are not having a dog and a cat in our wedding."

"Are you sure?" he asked. "It would definitely be memorable."

"Very sure," she said. "The only thing that needs to be that memorable about our wedding is that I get to become Mrs. Ryan Shepherd."

"'Mrs. Ryan Sheperd,'" Ryan repeated. "I kind of like the sound of that."

"I do, too," she said, smiling. "I can't wait."

A letter from the Author

To each and every one of my Amazing readers: *I hope you enjoyed this story as much as I enjoyed writing it. Let me know what you think by leaving a review!*
I'll be releasing another installment in two weeks so to stay in the loop (and to get free books and other fancy stuff) Join my Book club.

Stay Curious,
Susan Gillard